The Wise Bear Stories
Helping you through life's journey

Bullying: a new perspective

Scott Cranfield

Illustrations Raphilena Bonito

The Wise Bear Stories
Bullying: a new perspective
Scott Cranfield

Text and Illustrations © Scott Cranfield

ISBN 9781909660984

Published 2019
Tricorn Books
Aspex Gallery, 42 The Vulcan Building
Gunwharf Quays
Portsmouth PO1 3BF

Printed & bound in the UK

Bullying: a new perspective

How it Started:

Scott Cranfield the Author of Wise Bear has coached at the highest level for over 30 years, appearing on TV, radio, magazines, as well as hosting multiple seminars and being a key note speaker. His coaching covers subjects from life coaching and family relationships, to sport and business.

Since a young age I have been fascinated with and studied ways to help myself and others live the most inspired and fulfilled life possible. My journey has involved travelling the World attending countless programs and courses covering just about every area of life with the World's leading teachers.

As a father I wanted to share the best of what I had learnt with my children. I found a very effective way of doing this was through bedtime stories. I would create stories involving the challenges and anxieties my children had experienced that day and at the centre of each story is a character called Wise Bear. During the story the children would share with Wise Bear what was upsetting them or causing them to feel anxious. Wise Bear would use his vast experience and wisdom and share a whole new way of looking at these concerns to bring a calming balance to the children's mind, a balance they couldn't find on their own.

In each story the children learn useful tools and actions they can then apply for the rest of their lives.

My whole family are involved in bringing these stories to life, and it is our wish that these stories now help many other children and families, in the way they have helped ours.

Who is Wise Bear:

Wise Bear has been in the same family for generations. He has developed a unique wisdom that allows him to guide children, helping them dissolve their anxieties, as well as helping them make sense of the

different challenges and events they experience in their lives.
Every story covers a different subject, but within each story Wise Bear offers timeless lessons and vital life skills to help children navigate the journey of their life.

The lessons from Wise Bear will bring a calming balance to your children's mind, and give them a new and empowering perspective on any anxieties or challenges they face.

Even at 100 years old Wise Bear is still fascinated to learn and develop himself. He has had many brilliant teachers along the way, one special one he affectionately refers to as Dr D.

Wise Bear loves to read, exercise, make healthy smoothies and meditate. The only thing that gives away his age are some of his quirky sayings!

More than a story:
Each story ends with an affirmation and a short exercise to reinforce the lesson you have been reading about. This is a great opportunity to work with your children and help them apply the lessons directly to their own life.

Affirmations are a powerful way to develop strong and empowering beliefs for children, and the exercises give the children the opportunity to work through some of the challenges they face, so they can dissolve the anxieties and negative effects they hold in their mind.

Bullying: a new perspective

It had been a long day at school. The sun was shining and Toby and his sister, Alex, were looking forward to getting home. They sat in the back of the car, staring at the familiar houses as they drove by.

"How was school?" Mum asked.

Toby replied first, his face lighting up. "Really good! My teacher said I worked hard today. I'd remembered all my seven times table!"

"Wow! Well done, Toby," said Mum, smiling with pride.

They drove past the park. Toby and Alex craned their necks to see the other children swinging and sliding in the playground. They could hear the shrieks of delight as their classmates raced around together, moving eagerly towards the climbing frame.

Taking a deep breath, Alex shuffled awkwardly in her seat.

"And how about you, Alex? How was the school trip?" Mum looked at Alex in her rear-view mirror. Alex could see that she was still smiling, her eyes twinkling with happiness.

But Alex looked glum. She stared out of the window as the clouds drew in, casting a grey cloak over the houses.

"Not so good," she replied, sighing deeply.

She looked down into her lap, where her hand was fiddling nervously with the cuff of her dress.

The car drew to a halt at the traffic lights near their home. Mum turned around to look at Alex.

"Oh, what happened?" she said, a look of concern spreading across her face.

Alex sniffed, fighting back the tears.

"There are these children who aren't being very nice to me. They are being really mean and I don't like it."

She turned away, wiping her nose on her shoulder and staring intently at the pattern on the car seat.

Mum took a deep breath. "Are you sure, darling? Do you think that you might have misunderstood? I am sure that they didn't mean to be horrible. And I bet it will all be forgotten in the morning."

Mum was desperate to make Alex feel better.

But Alex did not feel better. She kicked the back of the seat to show Mum that she didn't think that it would all be OK tomorrow. Luckily, they soon arrived home and parked outside their neat terraced house.

"OK, OK," said Mum, opening the car door to let the children out. "Alex, I can see this is really upsetting you.

 Go and find Wise Bear to see if he can offer some advice."

"OK, Mummy," Alex replied, dragging her school bag along the gravel path and crashing through the front door.

"Oh and Alex!" Mum called out after her, as Alex stomped up the stairs. "While I remember, Grandma left you a message saying she was thinking about you and wanted to know how your school trip went. Can you call her back?"

"Yeah, OK," she replied, sounding slightly less glum at the prospect of speaking to Grandma.

Alex got to the top of the stairs and stopped outside Wise Bear's door. She could hear calming music coming from the room – pan pipes and soothing incantations.

She took a deep breath to compose herself then charged inside. By the window, stood Wise Bear, breathing deeply and practising his yoga. He was standing on one leg, his furry paws clasped together.

She couldn't hold herself back any longer. Alex took a couple of strides across the room and gave Wise Bear a huge hug, causing him to wobble.

"Oh golly! What do we have here?" Wise Bear exclaimed. "That's the hug of someone who isn't feeling quite right."

Tears were now flowing down Alex's face.

"What's the matter, Alex. Why are you crying?" asked Wise Bear.

Alex looked up to Wise Bear, her bottom lip quivering.

"The children at school are bullying me and teasing me," Alex blurted out, as she wiped her nose on the sleeve of her dress.

"Oh crikey! That doesn't sound good," he responded, planting his other foot firmly on the ground "Here, have a hankie and wipe your tears away."

Alex looked into his green eyes, hoping that Wise Bear would be able to lift her out of this sadness.

"Look Alex, I know it's not nice when someone is being mean to you but I want to share with you an important lesson that might help you for the rest of your life.

"It's some of the most important advice I can ever share with you. Would you like to hear it?"

Alex shuffled on her seat, and picked at some fluff on her socks.

"OK," she replied, catching her breath as her tears started to subside.

Wise Bear continued. "What I am going to share with you, very few people ever learn, which is a shame because it is a wonderful piece of guidance. It is something I learnt from Dr D.

"Alex, anytime you feel someone is being mean to you or challenging you, you can be sure that someone else is being kind to you or supporting you."

Alex looked a little confused and still upset. She didn't feel that anyone had been kind to her or helped her today.

"So, if you knew at the same time your friends were being mean to you, others were supporting you, how would that make you feel?"

Alex looked a bit confused, but thought for a moment and then said, "Well if that were true I would feel much better because I would know some people still like me, but today no one was being my friend – they were all mean to me."

Wise Bear continued.

"Alex, sometimes your mind can play tricks on you by making you believe things that aren't always true. It does this by only noticing half of the story. This lesson will help you see the whole story. And the whole story lets you know the truth.

"So, shall we see if we can find the other half of the story?"

Wise Bear now had Alex's full attention, but she didn't look convinced.

"OK," replied Alex reluctantly.

Wise Bear took a deep breath and looked directly at Alex. His chestnut whiskers quivered slightly as he spoke.

"Alex, I want you to close your eyes and in your mind, go back to the memory when your friends were bullying and teasing you."

Alex, now enthralled, did as she was told. She solemnly closed her eyes.

Wise Bear paused for a moment.
"Are you back in the memory?" he checked.

"Yes," said Alex softly, as her body began to relax.
"Great, so at the moment your friends were being mean,

who was supporting you?"

Alex's body jolted and she opened her eyes, glaring.

"No one was supporting me, they were all being mean!" she exclaimed crossly.

"**Goodness gracious me!**" said Wise Bear, quickly putting his woolly paw over his mouth, as he didn't mean to say that out loud. This made Alex smile.

Wise Bear shuffled in his seat and quickly got back to his point.

"Some people offer their support without saying anything, they are just thinking about you. They don't even need to be near you, but if you open your mind you will sense their support."

Wise Bear was quiet for a moment, so Alex could think about what he had said. After this short pause, he continued.

"Close your eyes again, and go back to the memory. Are you there?"

"Yes," said Alex, confidently.

"Good, now stay with the memory and ask your mind who was supporting you. You will know when you have found the answer because it will feel real," said Wise Bear.

After a few seconds, Alex opened her eyes looking a little startled, and said, "My best friend Emily."

"Are you sure?" asked Wise Bear.

"Yes, Emily was there when it happened. After they left, Emily gave me a hug and comforted me, and also Clara stayed back to see if I was OK."

Wise Bear was pleased. "Splendid, Alex, can you now see that even though Emily and Clara didn't say anything they were actually supporting you with their thoughts?"

"Yes, it's beginning to make sense," said Alex, sounding happier.

But Wise Bear hadn't finished his lesson.

"Alex, can you think of times when you have been supporting someone without actually saying anything?"

Alex paused for a moment. She looked to the ceiling as she thought carefully. After a few seconds, she turned again to Wise Bear, nodding slowly.

"Yes," said Alex. "That actually happens quite often. The other day I thought Dad was being too hard on Toby about not tidying his room. When Dad was telling Toby off, I was actually thinking that Toby had worked quite hard at looking after his room, but I was only thinking this, I didn't actually say anything."

"**Well done, Alex,**" said Wise Bear. "For you to learn that challenge and support always go together is a very important lesson."

"Challenge and support," Alex muttered to herself under her breath. "Yes, I understand!"

Wise Bear nodded sagely, and smiled to himself. She was a bright girl, that Alex, he thought.

"Oh! I need to call Grandma! Thank you so much, Wise Bear," she said as she gave him a big squeeze.

Alex went downstairs to the kitchen to make the phone call. Grandma answered the phone and said, "I'm so pleased to hear from you, I was having my lunch today and I was worried about you in case the school trip didn't go well with your friends. You know how sometimes there can be arguments on these trips."

Alex was amazed because it was lunchtime when she was being bullied. Alex realised it really was true what Wise Bear said. You can be supported by someone who is not even with you.

The following week Alex really enjoyed school. She was enjoying the lessons and having lots of fun with her friends.

Until sports day.

Alex had just done the long jump.

"Haha! That was a bit rubbish – can't you jump further than that?" taunted one of the boys in her class.

Alex started to get upset, but then quickly remembered what Wise Bear had said about challenge and support. She thought to herself that there must be support somewhere to balance this challenge. She looked around and noticed the sports teacher smiling at her. He called her over.

"Alex, you may not have won but do you realise that is the longest you have ever jumped? Well done, you should be very pleased with your effort!"

Alex thanked the teacher and couldn't resist a little smile to herself. From that day on, Alex felt very different knowing that she will never be in a situation where she is getting more challenge than support. All she needs to do is open her mind and take a look.

Wise Bear affirmation: What you say to yourself can make a big difference to how you think.
That's why Wise Bear always recommends an affirmation to help you remember his stories.
Here is today's one…

"I get challenge and support from my friends and family and it helps me to grow"

Wise Bear recommends repeating these affirmations regularly. You can say them either out loud or inside your head.

Wise Bear exercise:

Use the questions below to discuss with your children and family how Wise Bear thinking can help you.

Go through your memory and write below 10 examples of where you have received support at the same time as challenge, just like Alex did in this story. Often in a family, one parent will be challenging and the other will be supporting or a brother or sister might be playing opposite roles. You can use really recent situations or go back to memories from years ago.

Here is one example to start you off:

Situation when you were being challenged	Who was challenging you?	Who was supporting you, and how did they do it? Remember they are not always there, sometimes they are just in your mind.
My eldest brother took away my toy castle that I wanted to play with	Tom, my eldest brother	James, my younger brother, came and asked me to join in his game which was actually a lot of fun

Situation when you were being challenged	Who was challenging you?	Who was supporting you, and how did they do it? Remember they are not always there, sometimes they are just in your mind.

Situation when you were being challenged	Who was challenging you?	Who was supporting you, and how did they do it? Remember they are not always there, sometimes they are just in your mind.

The Wise Bear Stories

Helping you through life's journey